OLD MACDONALD

HAD A FARM

ILLUSTRATED BY CAROL JONES

Houghton Mifflin Company

l had a farm

-igh O

m he had a . . .

DO

Ee-igh

With a bark bark here,
Here a bark, there a bark,
Old MacDon

Ee-igh

Old MacDonald had a farm

Ee-igh Ee-igh O

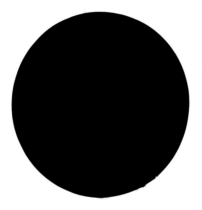

And on that farm he had a . . .

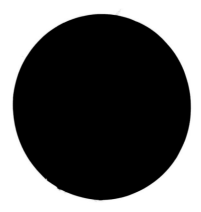

CHICKEN!

Ee-igh Ee-igh O

With a cluck cluck here, and a cluck cluck there
Here a cluck, there a cluck, everywhere a cluck cluck...
Old MacDonald had a farm

Ee-igh Ee-igh O

Old MacDonald had a farm

Ee-igh Ee-igh O

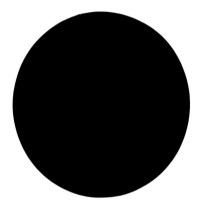

And on that farm he had a . . .

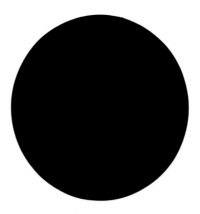

DUCK!

Ee-igh Ee-igh O

With a quack quack here, and a quack quack there
Here a quack, there a quack, everywhere a quack quack...
Old MacDonald had a farm

Ee-igh Ee-igh O

Old MacDonald had a farm

Ee-igh Ee-igh O

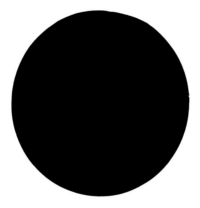

And on that farm he had a . . .

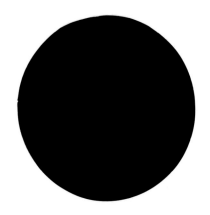

PIG!

Ee-igh Ee-igh O

With an oink oink here, and an oink oink there
Here an oink, there an oink, everywhere an oink oink . . .
Old MacDonald had a farm

Ee-igh Ee-igh O

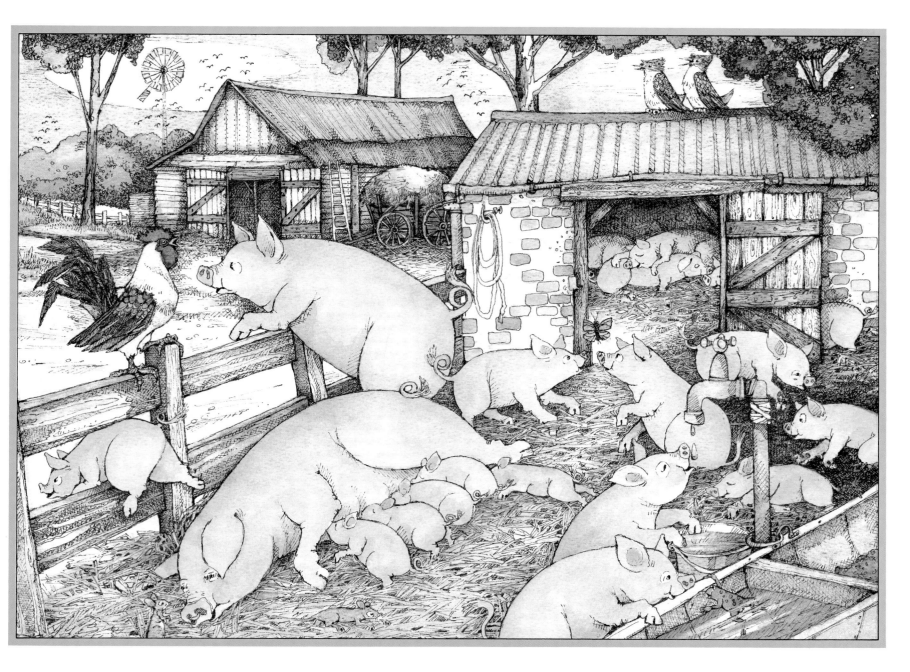

ald had a farm

Ee-igh O

rm he had a . . .

SHE

Ee-igh E

With a baa baa here,
Here a baa, there a baa, e
Old MacDonal

Ee-igh E

...nald had a farm

...a Ee-igh O

...farm he had a . . .

COW

Ee-igh Ee-

With a moo moo here, a
Here a moo, there a moo, eve
Old MacDonald

Ee-igh Ee-

Old MacDonald had a farm

Ee-igh Ee-igh O

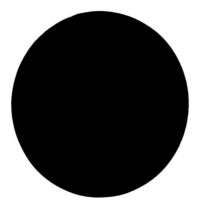

And on that farm he had a . . .

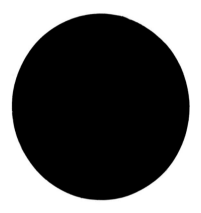

HORSE!

Ee-igh Ee-igh O

With a neigh neigh here, and a neigh neigh there
Here a neigh, there a neigh, everywhere a neigh neigh . . .
Old MacDonald had a farm

Ee-igh Ee-igh O

Old MacDonald had a farm

Ee-igh Ee-igh O

Walter Lorraine *uλ* Books

Library of Congress Cataloguing-in-Publication Data:

Old MacDonald had a farm/illustrated by Carol Jones.
     p.   cm.
     Summary: In this version of the familiar song, the reader is asked
to guess which animal comes next by looking through a peep hole.
     ISBN 0–395–49212-2(cl.).   ISBN 0-395-90125-1 (pbk.).
     1. Folk-songs, English–United States–Texts.
2. Toy and movable books–Specimens.
[1. Folk songs, American. 2. Toy and movable books.]
1. Jones, Carol, ill.
PZ8.3.042   1989
784.4'05–dc19   88-23269
               CIP
               AC

Illustrations copyright © 1988 by Carol Jones

First American edition 1989 by Houghton Mifflin Company

Originally published in Australia in 1988 by Angus&Robertson
now an imprint of HarperCollins*Publishers* Pty Limited
http://www.harpercollins.com.au
First published in the United Kingdom by Angus&Robertson (UK) in 1988

Printed in China

HCP 20 19 18 17 16 15 14

PO 4500252163